*This book
made possible
through generous gifts
to the
Nashville Public Library
Foundation Book Fund*

The Gryphon Press

—a voice for the voiceless—

These books are dedicated to those who foster compassion toward all animals.

For Nora Alleyn and Min — L. G-B.

To all who help improve the lives of tame and feral cats — N. L.

Printed in Canada by Friesens Corporation
Text set in Cochin by BookMobile Design and Publishing Services

Library of Congress Control Number: 2011933293
ISBN: 978-0-940719-12-5
1 3 5 7 9 10 8 6 4 2
A portion of profits from this book will be
donated to shelters and animal rescue societies.

I am the voice of the voiceless:
Through me, the dumb shall speak;
Till the deaf world's ear be made to hear
The cry of the wordless weak.

—from a poem by Ella Wheeler Wilcox, early 20th-century poet

KokoCat, Inside and Out

Lynda Graham-Barber • Nancy Lane

The Gryphon Press
–a voice for the voiceless–

KokoCat is an inside cat.
She stalks the sun around the room.

She bats the blinds and boxes with the velvet shadows.
She stares at the squirrel and swishes her tail.

She stretches and naps and preens and purrs.
KokoCat is warm, well fed, and loved.

One morning when the door opens,
KokoCat streaks outside.
"KokoCat, come back! Ko—ko—!"
KokoCat runs and runs and runs.
She runs until she no longer feels the sun.

A striped-orange tomcat slaps KokoCat flat onto her back.

Hungry, KokoCat licks a greasy bag on the ground.

She lunges at a bird . . . but the bird flies off.

Thirsty, she laps water from a sour puddle.

A shaggy, black-and-white dog chases KokoCat.
She darts across a noisy, crowded road.

Horns blow. Tires screech.

KokoCat races into an alley and squeezes under a garbage bin.
The hard shadows scare KokoCat.
KokoCat is cold, hungry, and alone.

Finally she falls asleep.
KokoCat dreams about . . .
her food bowl,
her warm window seat,
her soft spot on the bed.

"KokoCat, Ko — Ko,
where are you?"

The voices she knows
so well are near.

"KokoCat, you're dirty—and hurt."

Her family takes her to the veterinarian
to examine and treat her wounds.
The veterinarian gives KokoCat a shot
and rubs salve on her wounds.

Safe at home again,
KokoCat stretches
in the sunny window.

She grooms
her fur
clean and shiny.

KokoCat
is an indoor cat.
For good.

Keeping Your Cat Safe
for parents and other adults

Cat lovers know the pleasure cats bring to an individual or a family. Americans have enjoyed cats as pets since European colonists brought the first felines here hundreds of years ago. It's likely that shorthair cats were aboard the *Mayflower* working as mousers.

Estimates of the number of outdoor cats in the United States range from 80 to 120 million. That's one outdoor cat for every three people! This number includes pet cats that are allowed outside, those that are lost or abandoned, and feral or semiwild felines.

In the United States, 33 percent of people have a cat. Although 64 percent of those cats live strictly indoors, the question of whether a house cat should be allowed to roam outside is hotly debated. The life span of an outdoor cat averages four-and-a-half years, whereas the life expectancy of an indoor cat is around fourteen years.

Outside, cats fall victim to automobiles, dogs, wild animals, and diseases such as feline leukemia and rabies. All warm-blooded animals, including cats, can contract rabies and transmit it to other warm-blooded animals, including people.

As natural predators, even well-fed cats will hunt birds and small mammals. Although numbers vary widely, cats are responsible for killing millions of songbirds every year in the United States alone.

You can help protect both your cat and local wildlife by keeping your cat indoors. Scratching posts, carpeted tunnels, elevated perches, and catnip-laced toys are a few of the indoor-exercise options available.

To provide safe outdoor exercise for your cat, consider screening in a patio, building or buying an enclosure that's attached to your home, or fencing in part of your yard.

Make sure these enclosures are escape-proof, and your cat will be free to bask in the sun, exercise, and even stalk without posing a threat to wild creatures. It's important, however, that someone supervise confined cats, as they will be defenseless against intruding animals.

There's general agreement among experts that cat owners should provide a collar fitted with an identification tag for their pets. Make sure the collar is an approved breakaway style, which will minimize the risk of strangulation. Also, to avoid possible injury, never tie your cat to a fixed object.

On the final page, KokoCat is shown wearing an ID collar, one that will help ensure her future safety in the event she escapes from her owner and becomes lost. One resource to consider consulting if your cat is lost is http://www.missingpetpartnership.org.

Finally, consider KokoCat's adventure. Is she safer inside or outside?